Rub-down transfer book

Butterflies & Bugs

Illustrated by Bethan Janine

Designed by Emily Beevers, Mary Cartwright & Lucy Wain
Edited by Hannah Watson & Felicity Brooks

The transfers at the front of this book can be added
to the illustrated scenes on the right-hand pages.
There are tips on how to use them at the back of the book.
Use pens or crayons to decorate the left-hand pages.

In the Meadow

green shield bug

bluebottle fly

cardinal beetle

six-spot burnet moth

black garden ant

silver-sided sector spider

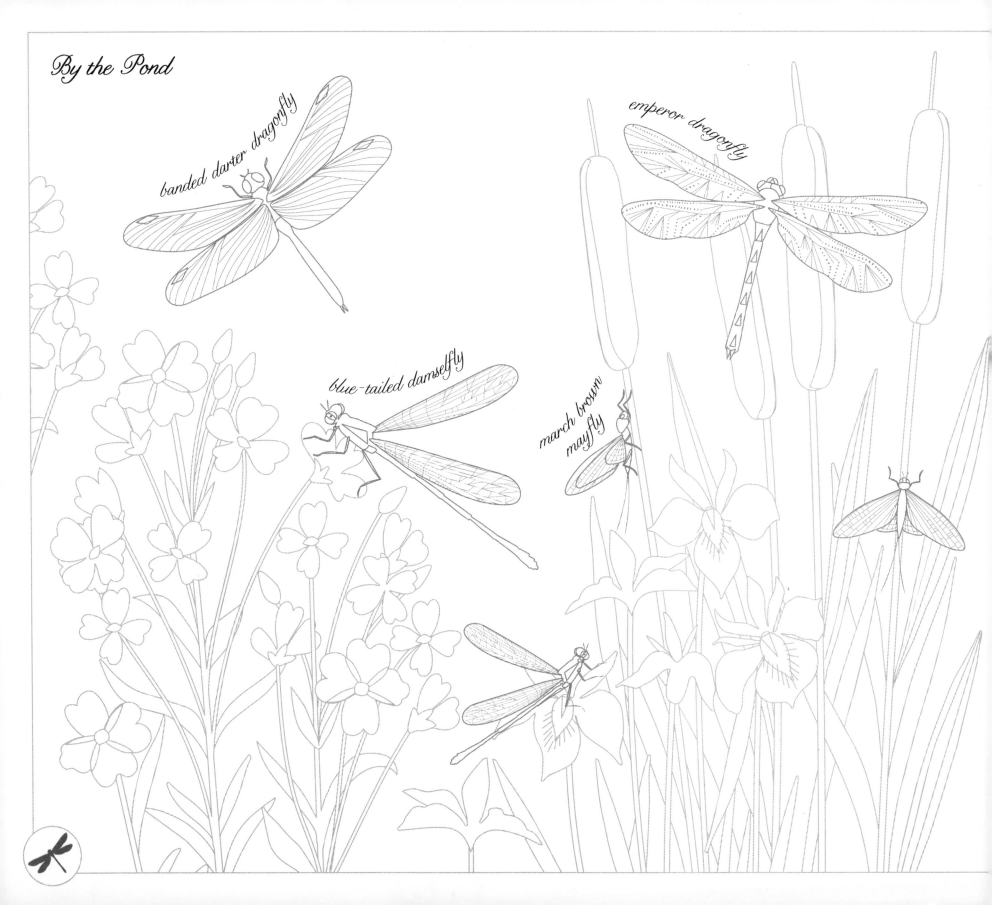

By the Pond

banded darter dragonfly

emperor dragonfly

blue-tailed damselfly

march brown mayfly

In the Jungle

agathina emperor

blue morpho

tailed sulphur

leafcutter ant

giant metallic ceiba borer

The Butterfly House

Indian leafwing

malachite

scarlet Mormon

banded orange

tiger longwing

The Forest Floor

common woodlouse

common earwig

lesser stag beetle

stone centipede

flat-backed millipede

grove snail

A Hedgerow

gatekeeper

purple emperor

holly blue

large skipper

stag beetle

ringlet

By the Shore

cloudless sulphur

Eastern tiger swallowtail

monarch

cow ant

large milkweed bug

cloudless sulphur caterpillar

monarch caterpillar

Honeybee Garden

dame's violet

Western honeybee

echinacea

A Farmhouse Wall

golden ground beetle

lace webbed spider

violet ground
beetle

garden snail

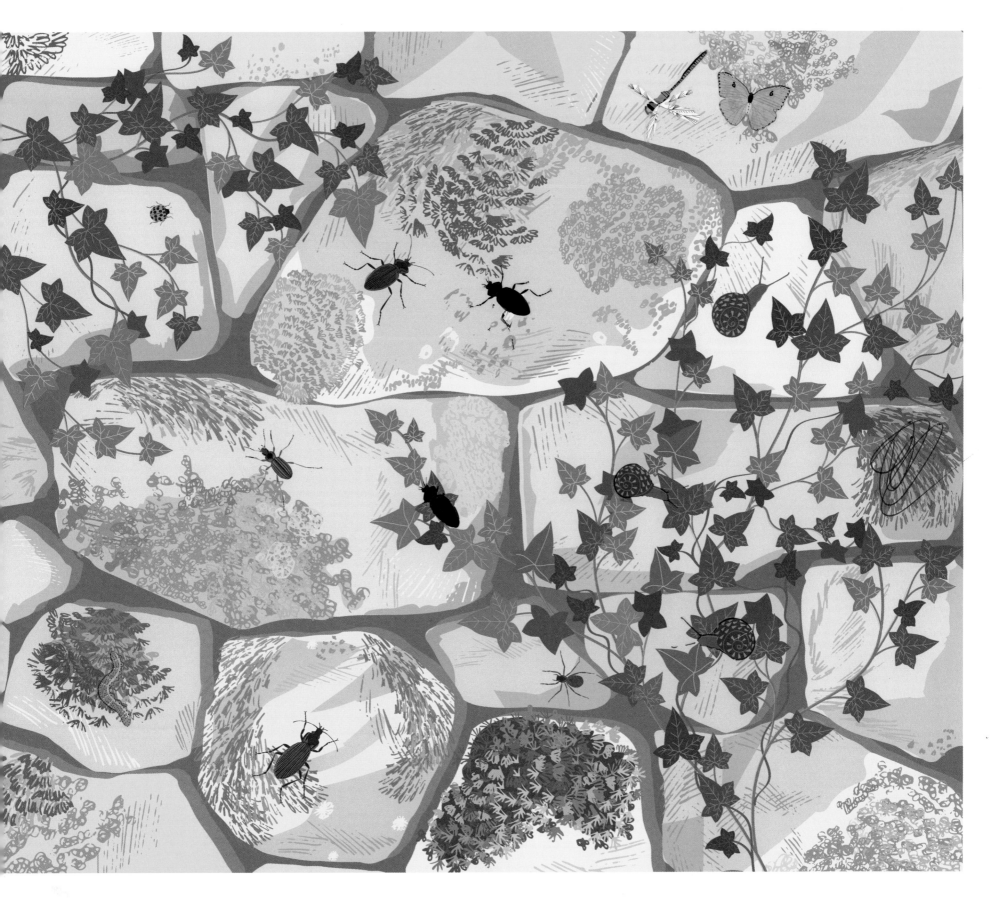

In the Orchard

comma

red mason bee

rose chafer
beetle

red admiral

orange-tip

speckled wood

Twilight
Garden

elephant hawkmoth

luna moth

brimstone moth

clouded
buff moth

privet hawkmoth

oleander hawkmoth

garden tiger moth

firefly

How to use this book

To fill the scenes with beautiful butterflies and bugs, you'll need a ballpoint pen or a pencil to add the rub-down transfers to the right-hand pages of this book. You can use crayons or felt-tip pens to decorate the left-hand pages.

Using the transfers

Take the transfer sheets out of their pocket and find the one with the symbol that exactly matches the symbol on the pages you want to work on. (Some sheets contain the transfers for two scenes.) Remove the backing sheet.

To use the transfers, position one of the little pictures over the place you want it to go in the scene.

Scribble all over it firmly with a pencil or ballpoint pen, taking care not to touch the pictures around it.

When you have completely covered the transfer, gently lift off the transfer sheet.

First published in 2017 by Usborne Publishing Ltd., Usborne House, 83-85 Saffron Hill, London EC1N 8RT, England. Printed in China.